Weekly Reader's Favorite Christmas Stories and Poems

(Formerly published as *Buddy's Favorite Christmas Stories and Poems*)

by the Staff of Weekly Reader

Edited by Elizabeth Zuraw

Weekly Reader Books
Middletown, Connecticut

Cover art by Jane Demelis
Text art by Jim Robison
Designed by Joyce Petersen

Publishing, Executive, and Editorial Offices:
Weekly Reader Books
Middletown, CT 06457

Weekly Reader's Favorite Christmas Stories and Poems

With acknowledgement to the following
members of the Weekly Reader staff:
Ann D. Hardy, Virginia H. Niles,
Pauline C. Peck, Constance Unsworth
and Pearl H. Watts.

With acknowledgement also to the following
authors whose stories and poems are
reprinted with permission:
Iris Just Adamson, Leland B. Jacobs,
VaDonna Jean Leaf, Sandra Liatsos and
Ruth McFadden Svec.

Table of Contents

STORIES

POEMS

Christmas Eve Magic

by Pauline C. Peck

Once upon a time, on a Christmas Eve, five funny clowns stood on a carousel in the window of a big building. They were all clowns from Santa's Circus.

There was Santa Claus Clown, Polka Dot Clown, Ruffle Plaid Clown, Jingle Bell Clown, and Holly Clown. The five clowns were all good friends.

People loaded down with bundles passed by the building and stopped to look at the carousel in the window.

"Look, Mom," shouted one little boy. "Look at the five funny clowns on the pretty

9

carousel. But why doesn't it turn around to music like other carousels?"

"I don't know," said the boy's mother, and they hurried off to finish their shopping.

The carousel did have pretty decorations, and it was a comfortable place for the clowns; but it did not go around and around. It just stood still, and there was no music playing.

"I wish we were turning around and around," said Jingle Bell. "I can see in only one direction, and I'm tired of looking at the same old things all the time."

"If we were turning," said Holly, "I could look out the window. There are so many pretty lights to see on Christmas Eve."

"Me too, me too," said Polka Dot. "I wish we could go around too."

"Ho, ho, ho," said Santa Claus Clown. "So you all want to go around and around, do you? Well, maybe I can do something about that. You know, on Christmas Eve Santa Claus has magic powers. He rides his sleigh over rooftops and delivers presents to girls and boys. Maybe a Santa Claus Clown has magic powers on Christmas Eve too. Let's see now."

And laying a finger aside of his nose— he closed his eyes, and what do you suppose?

Suddenly the clowns heard music. It was very soft at first, and then it became louder and louder. The carousel began to turn. It went slowly at first and then faster and faster. The five clowns were twirling around and around while the music played loud and clear.

"Hurray for Santa Claus Clown!" shouted Ruffle Plaid.

"I can see pretty lights out the window," said Holly. "Ooooh, how pretty!"

"I love going around and around," said Jingle Bell. "This is as much fun as I thought it might be."

"Wheee!" said Polka Dot. "We are really twirling."

"Thank you, Santa Claus Clown," said all the clowns. "We are all glad that you have magic powers on Christmas Eve. Now the carousel is fun."

So the carousel with the five happy clowns twirled around and around until the sky started to get light and the last star was gone. Then the carousel started to slow down, and the music began to get softer and softer until the carousel was standing still again and the music was gone. Now Christmas Day was here.

Some people walked by the window in the big building on Christmas Day, and they stopped to look at the pretty carousel. "How pretty," the clowns heard them say. "Look at the five clowns. Each one is dressed so differently. It really is a pretty carousel, but it's too bad that it is just standing still. It really should be twirling around and around with music playing loud and clear."

But the five clowns were not sad. They just stood still and smiled. They knew that they HAD twirled around and around all night long—with music playing loud and clear.

Christmas Everywhere

There's Christmas in the snowflakes,
There's Christmas in the clouds,
There's Christmas in the streets and shops
And Christmas in the crowds.
There's Christmas in the blustery winds,
There's Christmas in the air.
From everything that I can see,
There's Christmas everywhere!

—Leland B. Jacobs

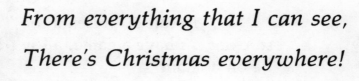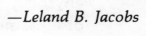

15

The Littlest Stocking

by Pauline C. Peck

It was Christmas Eve. The big house was still. Three stockings were hanging on the fireplace.

"I'm full of presents," said one of the stockings. "I have a ball and a doll and a tall candy cane."

"I'm full of presents too," said the second stocking. "I have a game, a toy train, and a whistle on a chain."

The third stocking was sad. It didn't say anything. The third stocking was the littlest one of all. And it was empty.

The stockings heard a noise. Someone

16

came down the chimney. He was dressed all in red. It was Santa Claus!

"Ho! Ho! Ho!" said Santa. "Where's the empty stocking?"

"Right here, sir," said the littlest stocking. "I'm hanging right here!"

Santa took something wiggly out of his pocket. Then he carefully put it into the littlest stocking.

"Ho! Ho! Ho!" said Santa. "Merry Christmas to all!" And he went back up the chimney!

The littlest stocking was happy. Now it had a present too. It had the littlest puppy in the whole wide world!

17

A Child Was Born

A little Child was born
One cold and wintery night,
And in the sky a silver star
Shone down with gleaming light.

The Child lay in a manger,
With cows and lambs close by,
While angels sang hosannas
That rang throughout the sky.

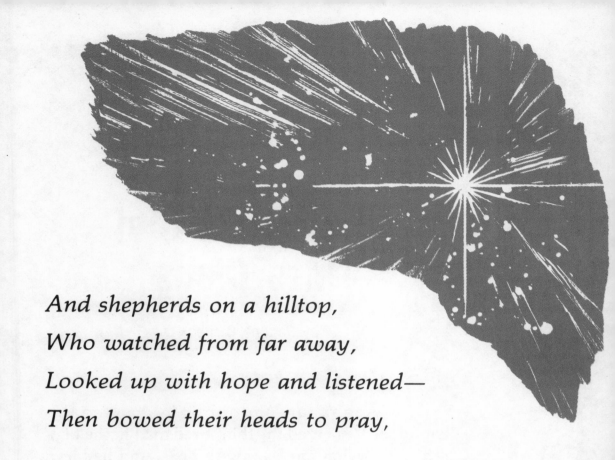

And shepherds on a hilltop,
Who watched from far away,
Looked up with hope and listened—
Then bowed their heads to pray,

That in the manger sleeping,
This Child of wondrous birth,
Would bring the joy of living
In peace, to all on earth.

—Pauline C. Peck

How Santa Met Mrs. Claus

by Pauline C. Peck

"Aaaaaaah-choooooo! Aaaaaaah-choooooo!" sneezed the thin, tired man in the big, red suit. "What am I going to do?" And he blew his bright red nose for the zillionth time.

Big, soft, white flakes were falling outside. The reindeer were all harnessed to the shiny, red sleigh. The huge pack was groaning full of toys and gifts. It was Christmas Eve. And poor Santa had a terrible, terrible cold!

Santa felt tired and sneezy and grumpy. He didn't feel jolly at all. And he didn't feel like going out.

20

Santa looked in his tall mirror. "Look at me," he said to his elves. "Just look at me. I look terrible. I feel terrible. My red suit is baggy in the knees. If I take a deep breath, my black belt will fall off. My hat is falling down over my eyes. And my red nose is so bright, I could lead the sleigh tonight!"

"Aaaaaaah-choooooo! Aaaaaaaaah-choooooooo! What am I going to do?" And he sat down in his rocking chair by the fire.

The tiny elves looked at one another. They were all thin and tired too. Everyone had been busy getting ready for Christmas Eve this year. They had worked harder than ever before. And no one had time to cook good meals.

Bong! Bong! Bong! Bong! The grandfather clock finished striking 12 times. It was midnight and time for Santa to go.

Santa sighed—a sniffly, wheezy sigh. He got slowly up out of his chair and started for the door. Poor Santa.

"I have to go," he told the elves. "Just think how the children would feel if Christmas didn't come this year. Why, they'd never believe in Santa again. But if I'm not back on time, send the North Pole Reindeer Patrol to find me."

"Merry Christmas, elves," he wheezed as he opened the door. Big swirls of cold, white flakes blew into the room. The elves shivered. Then the big door shut and Santa was gone.

The tired elves listened.
"On Donder, on Blitzen,"
they heard Santa say. Then
"Aaaaaaaaah-choooooo!
Aaaaaaaaah-choooooo!"
as the sleigh flew away.

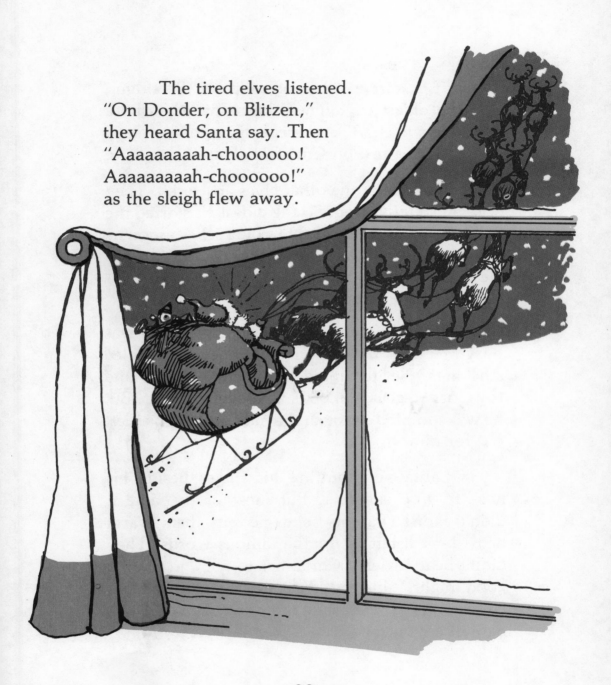

"I'll start a kettle of soup on the stove," said the oldest elf. "It will be ready when poor Santa gets back. Then he can sip some hot soup and get some rest on Christmas Day."

Not one of the other elves answered. They were all sound asleep. So the oldest elf started the soup and climbed into Santa's big rocker. Soon he was fast asleep too. Then all you could hear was the ticktock of the clock and z-z-z-z-z-z-z-z-z-z-z-z-z-'s as all the elves slept.

While the elves were sleeping, Santa was busy. He slid down sooty chimneys. He filled stockings. He decorated trees. He left gifts and toys for the girls and boys wherever he went. But he was too tired to touch the milk and cookies left out for him.

Santa kept putting his finger beside his nose to stop sneezing. But most of the time it didn't work. Parents, snuggled in their warm beds, kept listening for the famous words. They didn't hear, "Merry Christmas to all, and to all a good night." Instead they heard, "Aaaaaaaah-choooooooo! Aaaaaaaaah-choooooooo!" as Santa flew out of sight.

At last Santa had only one more home to visit. He was down to the very last name on his long list. The dark sky was beginning to grow light. The snow had almost stopped falling. And everything in sight was covered with a soft blanket of white.

"Whoa, Dancer! Whoa, Prancer!" called Santa hoarsely as they landed on the rooftop. He took the last gifts from his sack and went to the chimney.

Santa climbed into the chimney. It was a big chimney. Whoooooooooosh! Santa was so thin, he slid down too fast. He landed so hard, he saw stars. And the stars weren't in the sky!

"Who's there?" called a gentle voice from the kitchen. "Is that you, Santa Claus? You weren't supposed to stop here this year. My niece has gone to live with her grandmother. I'm all alone now." And she sighed a lonely sigh.

Santa shook his head to get rid of the stars. He looked up. There was the loveliest lady he had ever seen. Her blue eyes twinkled like the evening stars. She had round, rosy cheeks. And she smelled like fresh-baked bread!

"What's happened to you, Santa?" asked the lovely lady. "You look terrible. You're so thin you look like a scarecrow. And your nose is redder than Rudolph's. Hasn't anyone been taking care of you?"

"Aaaaaaaaah-choooooooo! Aaaaaaaaah-choooooooo!" answered Santa. And the last sneeze was the biggest of them all. It blew black, sooty ashes all over the lovely lady.

"I'm sorry," wheezed Santa. "I have a terrible cold. I'm sorry." And then be began to laugh. He laughed so hard that tears ran down his tired cheeks.

"Look at me?" chuckled Santa. "Take a look at yourself. My nose may be red, but yours is as black as my boots. I sneezed soot all over you!"

The lovely lady looked in the mirror. She did have a black, sooty nose!
She chuckled. She giggled.
Then she began to laugh too.
She laughed so hard that
she sat down beside Santa.
And they laughed together
by the black, sooty fireplace.

Back at the North Pole, something was wrong. The room was filled with smoke. The tiniest elf's nose twitched. He coughed and sputtered. He woke up rubbing his tiny eyes. When he saw the smoke, he shouted, "Wake up! Wake up!" to the other elves.

The rest of the elves woke up coughing and rubbing their eyes too. "It's the soup," shouted the oldest elf. "It's burning! Quick! Open the door!" And he grabbed the soup pot with two holders and put it safely out in the cold, wet snow. The hot pot sizzled and hissed in the snow.

"You woke up just in time," said the oldest elf. "Good for you, Tiny. You saved our lives. I wonder why Santa didn't wake up?" But Santa couldn't wake up because he was not there.

"Santa didn't come home," whispered the frightened elves. "Something must have happened to him. We'd better call the North Pole Reindeer Patrol."

Just then the elves heard something. They heard laughter coming nearer and nearer. They heard sneezes too. Was that Santa coming home at last? And why was he laughing?

The big door opened. In blew Santa, laughing and sneezing. And right behind him was . . . the loveliest lady the elves had ever seen.

"Elves," said Santa when he caught his breath. "I want you to meet someone. I want you to meet Mrs. Claus. We were married an hour ago by a sleepy man in a nightcap. We had to get him out of bed on Christmas Eve!" And for the first time in a long, long time, the elves heard Santa's jolly old "Ho, ho, ho! Ho, ho, ho!"

Mrs. Claus shooed everyone out of the kitchen, even Santa. Soon she had the kitchen clean and shiny again. And the kitchen smelled like fresh-baked bread and other goodies. Mrs. Claus was making a wonderful, tasty Christmas dinner.

After dinner that night, Santa and Mrs. Claus sat happily by the flickering fire. Santa winked at Mrs. Claus. "You're the best Christmas present I've ever had," he said.

Mrs. Claus smiled at Santa. "And I'm so happy with my big family. I'll never be lonely again," she answered.

Then both Clauses said, as they turned out the light, "Merry Christmas to all, and to all a good night!"

I'd Like To Be Santa Claus

I'd like to have his beard

And roly-poly nose.

I'd like to drive his sleigh

And wear his furry clothes.

I'd dive down the chimneys

And never would get stuck.

I'd bring special goodies

And lots of Christmas luck.

—Sandra Liatsos

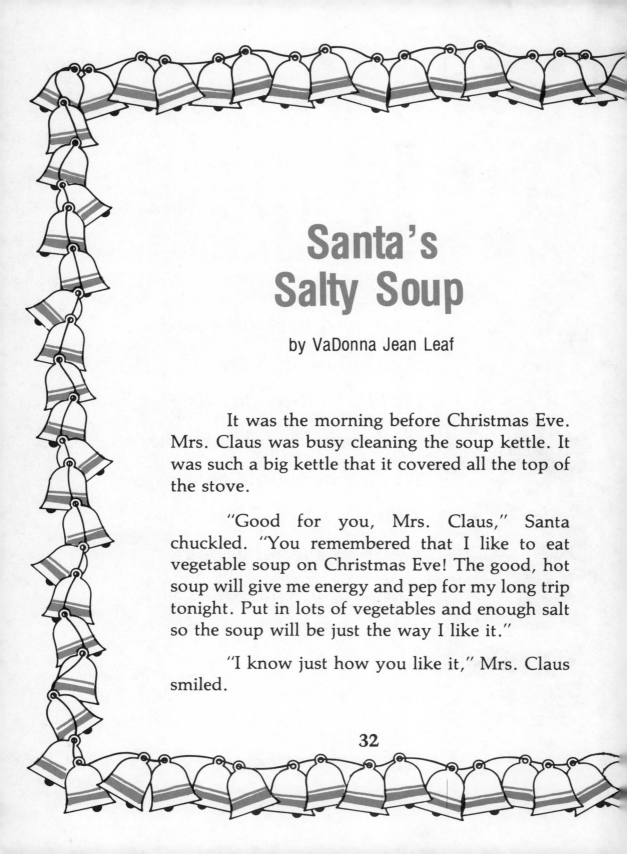

Santa's Salty Soup

by VaDonna Jean Leaf

It was the morning before Christmas Eve. Mrs. Claus was busy cleaning the soup kettle. It was such a big kettle that it covered all the top of the stove.

"Good for you, Mrs. Claus," Santa chuckled. "You remembered that I like to eat vegetable soup on Christmas Eve! The good, hot soup will give me energy and pep for my long trip tonight. Put in lots of vegetables and enough salt so the soup will be just the way I like it."

"I know just how you like it," Mrs. Claus smiled.

32

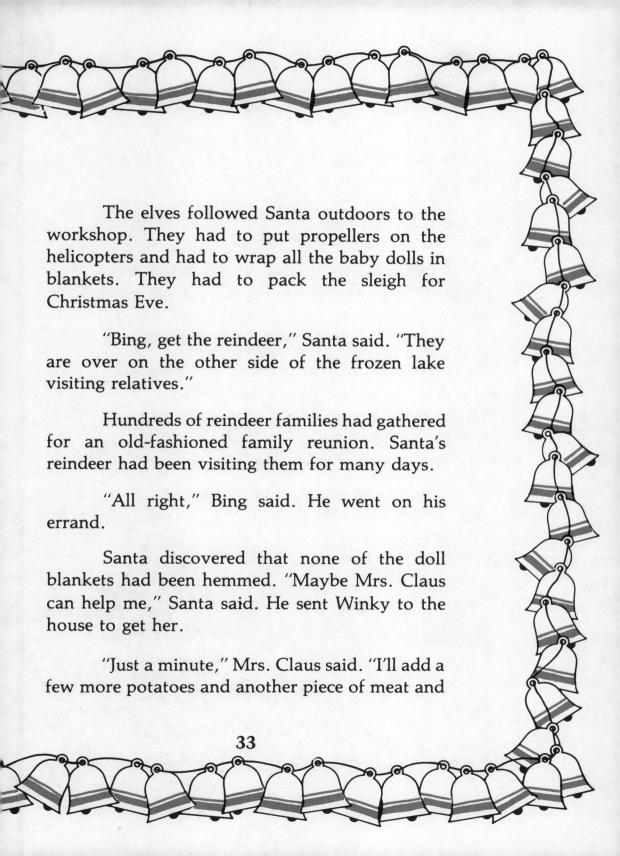

The elves followed Santa outdoors to the workshop. They had to put propellers on the helicopters and had to wrap all the baby dolls in blankets. They had to pack the sleigh for Christmas Eve.

"Bing, get the reindeer," Santa said. "They are over on the other side of the frozen lake visiting relatives."

Hundreds of reindeer families had gathered for an old-fashioned family reunion. Santa's reindeer had been visiting them for many days.

"All right," Bing said. He went on his errand.

Santa discovered that none of the doll blankets had been hemmed. "Maybe Mrs. Claus can help me," Santa said. He sent Winky to the house to get her.

"Just a minute," Mrs. Claus said. "I'll add a few more potatoes and another piece of meat and a little more salt to the soup. I want it to be just the way Santa likes it."

Mrs. Claus hurried out to the workshop. She started to hem doll blankets.

Tinkles went to the house to get more thread. He checked on the soup. "I'll put some beans and a little more salt into the soup," he said. "I want it to be just the way Santa likes it."

After a while Dusty went to the house to get a drink of water. He checked the soup. "I'll put cabbage and a little more salt into the soup," he said. "I want it to be just the way Santa likes it."

Later Buzz went in the house to get a Band-Aid. "I'll put corn and a little more salt into the soup," he said. "I want it to be just the way Santa likes it."

All day long Santa and Mrs. Claus and the elves worked hard. They didn't have time to eat dinner.

The soup cooked and bubbled on the stove. It sent good smells to the workshop. During the afternoon whenever the elves went to the house for something, they checked the soup. Each one added noodles or peas or tomatoes to the soup. And each one added just a little more salt so it would be just the way Santa liked it.

It was four o'clock. All the work in the workshop was done. Mrs. Claus and the elves were packing the sleigh.

Bing came running across the fields. "Come quickly! All the reindeer are sick!" Bing cried.

Santa and Mrs. Claus and all the elves hurried across the snow, up and down hills, and over the frozen lake.

All the reindeer were lying on the ground. They were very weak. They couldn't get up.

Santa patted Donder and Blitzen.

"What is wrong?" Bing asked. "Do they have snow fever or icicle pox?"

"Hmmm," Santa said. "It looks like the reindeer haven't been eating enough salt. Winky, haven't you been bringing salt to the reindeer?"

"I'm sorry, Santa." Winky hung his head. "We've been out of salt for many days. We've been so busy in the workshop that I forgot to order more salt."

"No salt? This is serious," said Santa.

"What about the salt in Mrs. Claus's pantry?" asked Blink.

"My salt is gone too," Mrs. Claus said. "It is such a strange thing. Just a few minutes ago I went into the house. I was going to put salt into the soup so it would be just the way Santa likes it. But the salt box was empty."

"Will the reindeer be all right?" asked Giggles.

"They will be all right as soon as they get some salt," Santa said. "But it takes many hours to go to town and buy salt. The reindeer will not be able to pull the sleigh tonight. And this is Christmas Eve."

Each one had tears in his eyes as he went back to the house. Santa had never failed the children before. Santa felt terrible. He did not want to eat his supper.

"Come," Mrs. Claus said. "This will make you feel better." She dished up big bowls of vegetable soup. She set big plates of crackers on the table.

Santa tasted his soup. "This soup is NOT the way I like it!"

All the elves tasted their soup. "This soup is too salty," they said.

"Oh, dear! I just put enough salt so it would be just the way Santa likes it," Mrs. Claus said.

"I put some salt in the soup," Tinkles said in a low voice.

"Me too," said Dusty.

"Me three," said Buzz.

All the elves admitted that they had salted the soup too.

"Oh, dear," Mrs. Claus said sadly.

"It is perfect soup!" Santa cried. "Quick, quick, help me carry the soup kettle outside!"

The elves didn't know what Santa wanted

them to do, but they carried the big kettle of soup outdoors. They loaded it onto Santa's sled and pulled the sled across the fields and up and down the hills and across the frozen lake. The soup cooled in the freezing air.

Santa stopped at the reindeer reunion. The elves helped Santa pour the soup into big feeding pans. They brought the pans to the reindeer. The reindeer began to drink and eat.

They started to feel better. The soup was salty enough to make the reindeer feel fine again. The meat and vegetables gave them energy.

"Christmas Eve is saved by Santa's Salty Soup!" shouted the elves.

They hurried home. The elves hitched the reindeer to the sleigh. Mrs. Claus made some sandwiches for Santa to eat.

Soon Santa was on his way with toys for all the boys and girls. "Merry Christmas! Merry Christmas!" he called.

Listen to Christmas

Christmas sounds
    are quiet sounds.
Secrets everywhere!
    Whisper sounds
       Sneaking sounds
Going here and there!

Christmas sounds
    are noisy sounds.
Everyone is gay!
    Happy sounds,
        Merry sounds!
Santa's on his way!

          —Pearl H. Watts

Wheezer the Sneezer

by Iris Just Adamson

Wheezer put another dab of polish on the toe of Santa's boot. The look on his face was as sad as could be. It was bad enough to be the smallest elf in Santa's work force, but to have a sneeze that shook the whole North Pole made it even worse. While all the other elves were downstairs doing fun things for Santa, he was made to stay upstairs with only the most uninteresting things to do. It wasn't his fault that he had an allergy that made him sneeze till he shook the toys off the shelves and sent Christmas tree decorations crashing to the floor. It was terrible when he sneezed and sent the gingerbread men all over the floor just as Mrs. Claus was taking them from the oven. A tear dropped from his little, red nose, and he wiped it off with his hand, getting a big blob of shoe polish on his cheek.

Later, when Santa came into the room with a huge sack of letters for Wheezer to open, things seemed a little brighter. But all the letters were from people who wanted snow for Christmas. Snow is one thing that Santa can't bring, although he lives in the midst of it.

There were letters from boys who wanted
new sleds,

And letters from farmers with dry watersheds.

Letters from skiers with idle ski lifts,

And letters from skiers who wanted some drifts.

Letters from mothers who were tired of mud,

And letters from nurserymen with trees all in bud.

Letters from salesmen with sleds and with skates,

And lots of toboggans all tied up in crates.

All were unhappy and mostly unreasonable.

Without any snow it was very unseasonable.

45

Wheezer read the long list
of complaints to Santa.
He sneezed only once,
and he blew the letters
from the floor
to the rafters.
How he wished
he could make
everyone
happy!

The day before Christmas, Wheezer sneaked down the stairs far enough to watch all the fun and excitement in the workroom below. How he longed to be a part of the fun! A tiny scrap of fuzz from a toy lamb floated toward him, and he rushed back up the stairs to his room. He sneezed and the whole house shook. "Take it easy up there!" someone shouted from below. "You almost spoiled Christmas for everyone!"

Poor Wheezer walked sadly over to the window. He looked through his tears at the other elves bringing in the reindeer to hitch to the bulging sleigh. Wheezer could see the bright glow of Rudolph's nose as he was led to the front of the line. Just then the door opened, and Santa stepped into the room to change into his new red suit. He looked at the boots that Wheezer had polished so carefully. Then he turned to look thoughtfully at the little elf.

"Wheezer," he said, with a smile, "how would you like to come with me tonight? You've missed a lot of fun this year. Come along and help me check the list."

Wheezer was overcome with joy. He bounced to the closet and pulled on his heavy coat and gloves. In a minute he climbed up on Santa's shoulder, and they were off to settle themselves in the sleigh for the happiest flight of the year. The other elves jeered when they saw Wheezer, and warned Santa that one sneeze would knock all the toys out of the sleigh. Santa only laughed as they started out into the cold, frosty night.

The stars twinkled merrily as they sped along over the endless sky, but suddenly the air became warmer; and big, fleecy clouds as soft as kitten fur were piled high on every side. It was a shame that those clouds couldn't let go of their loads of snow to make people happy, thought Wheezer. He snuggled close to Santa's shoulder. Suddenly the fur on Santa's collar tickled Wheezer on the nose. He held his breath. He pressed his finger tightly against his upper lip. He held both hands over his mouth. But nothing helped. His tiny body shook, and out came the sneeze more fiercely than ever before. He waited for Santa to scold him, but instead Santa shouted with joy! Falling from the big, feathery clouds were millions of huge, fluffy snowflakes!

It was snowing on boys who wanted new sleds.

It was filling the farmers' dry watersheds.

It was falling on skiers' shiny new lifts.

It was giving the skiers plenty of drifts.

It was giving the mothers something better
than mud.

It was letting trees rest that had started to bud.

Now salesmen would sell all the sleds and the
skates,

And even toboggans tied up in their crates.

With fluffy, white snow it made everything
seasonable!

Everyone would be happy and no longer
unreasonable!

Santa shouted happily, "You've saved the day, Wheezer! That sneeze was all those clouds needed to put down a blanket of snow! You're a hero, Wheezer!" At last, Wheezer had found his place in Santa's world.

I Wonder

I have a baby brother
Who sometimes cries at night
And keeps the family all awake
Until it's nearly light.

When Jesus was a baby
Do you think that Mary too,
Was wakened when He cried at night
The way most babies do?

—Ruth McFadden Svec

How
Santa Grew Fat

by Pauline C. Peck

A long, long time ago Santa Claus wasn't fat. He didn't have a round, little belly that shook when he laughed like a bowl full of jelly. And he wasn't jolly. Santa Claus was thin and sad. In fact, he was so thin and sad, he looked as though he hadn't eaten for a long time. He didn't look like the Santa we know today.

All during the year Santa worked hard making Christmas gifts for girls and boys. He had no helpers. He worked all day, and sometimes he worked until late at night. He had to work very hard to be ready for Christmas Eve.

On Christmas Eve, when it was time to deliver the gifts to good girls and boys, Santa had to walk! He didn't have a sleigh, and reindeer to pull it. Instead, Santa walked and walked carrying his sack of holiday goodies. He walked down winding roads and up high hills. He walked until the last gift was delivered and his big sack was empty. He walked until the stars were gone and it was Christmas morning. And then he walked back to his lonely home at the North Pole.

So you see, that's why Santa Claus wasn't fat. He worked so hard, he never had time to get fat. He didn't have time to eat a good dinner every day. He didn't have time to relax in his big chair by the fire. And on Christmas Eve he walked so far and so fast, he didn't even have time to eat the good foods that children put out for him. There was no way that he could be a jolly, plump, old elf.

Then one day something magical happened to change Santa's life. Suddenly elves appeared to help him in his workshop. They sang and they laughed as they helped Santa make his gifts. He didn't have to work so hard anymore. The elves made delicious dinners for Santa to eat. And after dinner they made him rest in his big chair by the fire. Santa was not lonely anymore.

And Santa began to grow fat. He soon had a round, little belly. His beard grew thick and white. He was so happy, he whistled while he worked. He smacked his lips when he ate the elves' delicious dinners. He snored happily when he snoozed in his big chair by the fire. And he grew fatter and fatter and jollier and jollier.

At last it
was Christmas Eve. Santa
put on a new, red suit
with white fur. He
pulled on shiny,
black boots
and a
warm,
furry,
red hat.
He filled
his big sack
with all the
children's gifts
he and the elves
had made. He lifted
the sack to his shoulder
and started to leave
on his long trip. But
something was wrong. The sack was
heavier than ever before. And Santa
was fatter than ever before. He was just
too fat to carry the heavy sack of gifts to
all the children's homes on Christmas Eve.

57

"Oh, dear," said Santa to his elves. "Now what do I do? I can't disappoint the children on Christmas Eve. What ever will I do now?"

But something magical was still happening. "Look outside, Santa," shouted the elves in their tiny voices. "Look outside." Santa opened the door and looked out into the dark, snowy night. There stood a beautiful, red sleigh and eight tiny reindeer. They were waiting to take Santa on his Christmas Eve ride. Santa did not have to walk!

Santa and his reindeer had a wonderful time that Christmas Eve. They flew over the snow with bells jingling wherever they went. They left gifts at the homes of all the good girls and boys. And Santa had time at each house to taste the yummy foods the children had put out for him.

59

At last it was Christmas morning. Santa and his reindeer were safely back at the North Pole. The reindeer were having their Christmas brunch of carrots and hay. Santa was relaxing in his big chair by the fire. He was telling the elves about the little, old man in his nightcap who had poked his head out of a bedroom window to see what was going on when he heard Santa and his reindeer. Santa was laughing so hard as he told his story, his round, little belly was shaking like a bowl of Christmas jelly! Santa was really happy.

Now all that happened a long time ago, long before you and I were born. Ever since then Santa Claus has been a plump, jolly, old elf. Sometimes the elves talk about putting Santa on a diet, but the children like him just the way he is. So he works and eats, snoozes and snores, and rides his sleigh full of toys for girls and boys every Christmas Eve. And he's the fattest and jolliest elf at the North Pole!

The magic that made Santa fat and jolly was the magic of words and pictures. In the poem "The Night Before Christmas," a man named Clement Moore used wonderful words to make Santa into the jolly, old elf that we all know and love.

Years later another man, Thomas Nast, read the Christmas poem and liked the jolly, plump Santa so much, he just had to draw him.

No one ever remembers the thin, tired Santa anymore. Santa is always jolly and fat now. So you see, there really is magic in words and pictures. It's a special kind of magic that brings Santa into the hearts of children everywhere.

Trim the Christmas Tree

Let's trim the Christmas tree!
Make some paper chains.
Cut a row of paper dolls
And get some candy canes.

String some snowy popcorn.

Paint some pine cones bright

And don't forget a golden star

To glow with Christmas light.

—*Pearl H. Watts*

Why the Christmas Tree Has Tinsel

by Pauline C. Peck

Once upon a time in a little town in Finland, a mother and her three children lived in a little cottage. The cottage was on the edge of a big forest. The family was very poor. So the owner of the forest let them cut down trees to burn in the fireplace to keep warm.

Christmas was coming, and the family had no money for gifts. "What shall we do for Christmas?" asked Eric, the younger boy. "It wouldn't be Christmas without gifts."

"Well," said Mother. "Why don't we each make a gift? That way we'll be giving gifts of love."

"I'll carve a whistle," said Karl, the older boy. "I'm good at carving whistles."

"I'll knit some mittens," said Kristen, the boys' sister. "I know where there is some leftover yarn."

"And I'll make a necklace of dried berries," said Eric. "I can use some of the berries that we saved to trim our Christmas tree."

"That's fine," said Mother. "And I'll make a batch of spicy cookies. We always enjoy cookies at Christmastime." And so the family was happy getting ready for Christmas.

On the day before Christmas the whole family went into the forest to find a Christmas tree. They looked and looked, but most trees were too big for their little cottage. At last they found a small tree. It didn't have many branches, but it would fit into their little cottage. Karl chopped it down with his ax, and the family carried it home through the snow. They put the tree in front of a window in the main room of the cottage. Everyone helped to decorate the tree. Strings of berries wound around the tree made it look bright and cheery. It wasn't the most beautiful Christmas tree in the world, but it was their tree. The family put the gifts they had made under the tree and climbed the ladder to the attic where they slept.

66

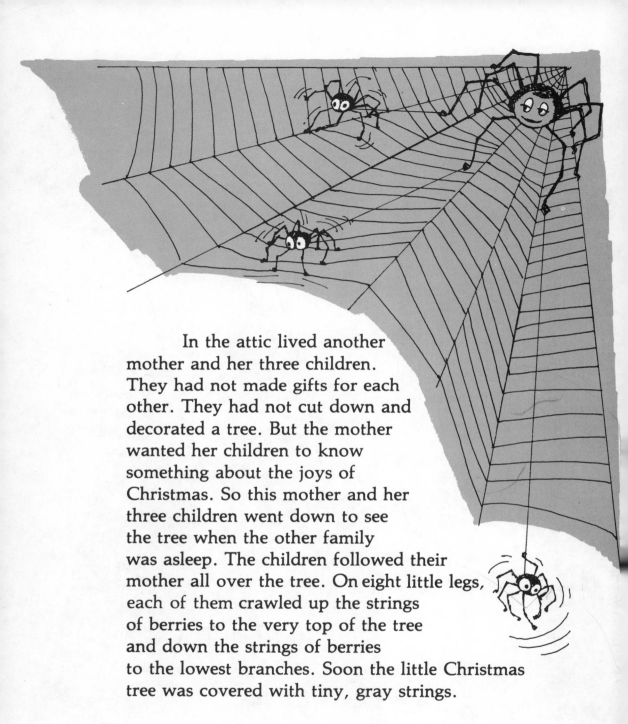

In the attic lived another
mother and her three children.
They had not made gifts for each
other. They had not cut down and
decorated a tree. But the mother
wanted her children to know
something about the joys of
Christmas. So this mother and her
three children went down to see
the tree when the other family
was asleep. The children followed their
mother all over the tree. On eight little legs,
each of them crawled up the strings
of berries to the very top of the tree
and down the strings of berries
to the lowest branches. Soon the little Christmas
tree was covered with tiny, gray strings.

Suddenly a light shone in the room. It was the Christmas Fairy. She had come to see if the Christmas gifts under the tree were given with love. She saw the tree covered with the thin, gray strings. Then she saw the mother and her babies. "Why, Mother Spider," said the Christmas Fairy, "what have you and your children done to the tree? You have covered it with spiderwebs."

Mother Spider looked at the tree. She saw all the webs she and her children had made. "Oh

70

dear! I'm so sorry," said Mother Spider. "But because I love my children so, I wanted them to know some of the joys of Christmas. We didn't mean to hurt the tree."

The Christmas Fairy smiled. "You gave your children a gift of love," she said. And she touched the top of the tree with her wand. Suddenly the tree was shiny and sparkling. The gray strings of webs were changed into strings of bright tinsel. It was a beautiful tree!

On Christmas morning, Karl, Kristen, and Eric came down from the attic to open their gifts. "Look!" called Eric. "Look at our beautiful tree."

"It looks so different," said Karl.

"Oh, yes," said Kristen. "Now it's the most beautiful tree in the whole wide world!"

And up in a corner of the attic Mother Spider smiled. She and her babies knew that the Christmas Fairy had made the tree beautiful. She had made it beautiful because of the gifts of love of the two families. And that is how the Christmas tree came to have tinsel.

"I am going to a party,"
Said a little Christmas tree,
"My jewels are bright and shining.
I'm as happy as can be.
        I will give each child a present
        Wrapped in paper bright and gay,
        And I'll whisper in my branches,
        'Have a happy Christmas Day.'"

—Pearl H. Watts

72

Lonnie, the Lonely Little Snowbird

by VaDonna Jean Leaf

Burr-rrr-rrr-ing! The alarm clock rang.

"Oh, how hard it is to wake up in the morning!" Santa said.

"It's a good thing you have an alarm clock to wake you," Mrs. Claus laughed.

Santa leaped out of bed and turned off the alarm clock. "I can't get along without this old clock."

"Especially at Christmastime," agreed Mrs. Claus.

73

"Listen," said Santa. "The snowbirds are waking up!"

The snowbirds sang a soft, twittering trill. They sang "Frosty the Snowman" and "Jingle Bells."

Jenny Snowbird sang a solo. She sang "Rudolph the Red-Nosed Reindeer." She made it full of lovely chirps and twitters.

"Beautiful!" Santa clapped his hands. Then Santa noticed one little gray snowbird sitting away by himself. His feathers drooped and his head hung low.

"Who is that?" Santa pointed.

"That is Lonnie, the lonely little snowbird," said Mrs. Claus.

"Why is he lonely?" asked Santa.

"Lonnie is lonely because he can't sing."

"Can't sing!" exclaimed Santa. "Everybody can sing, especially at Christmastime. Lonnie!" Santa called. "Come here."

Lonnie flew to Santa's windowsill.

"Yes, sir, Santa, sir," Lonnie whispered.

"Sing!"

"Oh, sir, Santa, sir," begged Lonnie.

"Sing 'We Wish You a Merry Christmas.' Everybody knows that song," Santa said.

Lonnie opened his tiny beak. "Burr-rrr-hhh-jerer-rrr!" sang Lonnie.

Mrs. Claus put her hands over her ears. The snowbirds hid their heads under their wings.

"Is that the best you can do?" Santa asked kindly.

"Yes, sir, Santa, sir."

"Lonnie is hopeless," Jenny Snowbird said. "Poor Lonnie. I don't think he'll ever learn to sing."

"It won't do, especially at Christmastime!" Santa said. He thought and thought. "I'll have my elves make a song box! With batteries! You can

carry it around your neck. Whenever you want to sing, you can flip the switch."

"Santa, sir, I don't want a song box."

"Don't want it! Don't you want to sing?"

"Oh, yes! My grandest wish in all the world is to be useful and important and to make you happy, Santa. But a song box—well, you see, Santa, sir, it wouldn't be really me."

"Hmmm," said Santa.

"Santa," Mrs. Claus interrupted. "Breakfast is ready."

77

"I must study this problem," answered Santa. "Lonnie must not be lonely, especially at Christmastime."

"That's just it, Santa," said Mrs. Claus. "It's the day before Christmas. We have lots of work to do."

"Yes, I must be ready for Christmas Eve," agreed Santa. He went to breakfast.

Santa and Mrs. Claus and the elves worked hard all day. Santa thought and thought about Lonnie.

"I can't think of anything to help Lonnie, the lonely little snowbird," Santa said when it was time for his nap. He started to wind the alarm clock.

Brr-thum-jing-zoo-yuk-yuk-yuk! The clock made a strange noise.

"The alarm clock is broken!" Santa exclaimed. "I can't wake up without it. And I need a little nap!"

"Are there any alarm clocks in your Christmas pack?" asked Mrs. Claus.

"There isn't another alarm clock in all the North Pole," Santa said.

"Can the elves make one?" asked Mrs. Claus.

"No," Santa said. "We've been so busy making presents. There aren't any supplies left!"

"You take your nap," said Mrs. Claus. "At just the right time, the elves and I will wake you."

Santa lay down on the bed and fell asleep.

Mrs. Claus called the elves. They were sleepy and sat around the room yawning.

The snowbirds sat on the roof. They would watch the time for Santa. Lonnie sat on the windowsill. He was so-o-o sad. He wanted to help too.

The elves fell asleep. Mrs. Claus tried to stay awake, but finally her eyes shut too. One by one the snowbirds tucked their heads under their wings.

Everybody went to sleep except Lonnie. Suddenly he knew it was time for Santa's Christmas Eve trip!

Lonnie pecked on the window. It was such a little sound. Santa did not wake up. Lonnie flew to the roof. He woke the snowbirds. They began to sing. But Santa did not wake up.

"I'll sing a solo," Jenny Snowbird said. She sang "Jingle Bells." She held the high notes loud and clear. But Santa did not wake up.

"I'll wake Santa!" Lonnie exclaimed.

"You! You sound like a donkey with a sore throat," scoffed the snowbirds.

"That's just it!" Lonnie said. He hopped close to the window. He took a deep breath.

"Burr-burrr-hhh-jerer-rrr!"
sang Lonnie.

Santa heard it. "It's time
for Christmas Eve!" Santa shouted,
jumping out of bed.

"Who made that awful
noise?" cried the elves.

"Who woke us up?"
cried Mrs. Claus.

"Oh, Santa, sir," Jenny Snowbird pecked on the window. "Lonnie woke you."

"Lonnie, the lonely little snowbird, saved Christmas Eve!" Santa exclaimed. "You see— *everybody can do something special.* Lonnie shall be my alarm clock. He must wake me every morning—and especially when I take a nap on Christmas Eve. It's an important job. Can you do it, Lonnie?"

"Oh, yes, sir, Santa, sir!" Lonnie exclaimed.

Santa got into his sleigh and flew through the air. "Merry Christmas to all!" he called.

"Merry Christmas!" sang the snowbirds. Then they sang a new song. "Lonnie, the lucky little snowbird, will never be lonely again! Not ever!"

It's Christmastime

Winter birds soar
in the heavens above
singing a song
of peace and of love—
What do they sing
so loud and so clear?
It's Christmastime—
Baby Jesus is here!

—Constance Unsworth

The Magic of the Holidays

by Ann D. Hardy

It was 5 o'clock when Mr. McAndrew finished hanging the last of the holiday decorations in his Teddies and Toys shop. He had worked very hard, and now it was time to go home. Before leaving the shop, Mr. McAndrew quickly checked to see that all the decorations were in place. Tinsel, bells, and ornaments adorned the teddy bears and toys. Everything looked perfect. Mr. McAndrew got his coat and hat, turned off the lights, and locked the door. He walked past the front window, giving it a last glance. Suddenly he stopped. Something was missing. *What was it?* he wondered. He had remembered Teddy

Bear, Jolly Clown, and Mrs. Mouse. Elf was on the mantle, Monkey was on his rope, the toys were under the tree—but something was missing. Too tired to go back into the store, Mr. McAndrew continued on his way.

The snow fell softly as Mr. McAndrew walked home. He could not get the missing something out of his mind. All the way home he stroked his beard and scratched his neck. *What did I forget?* he asked himself. *What could it be?*

When he got home, he ate dinner and then settled into his easy chair. The missing something was still on his mind, but he soon fell asleep.

All was quiet in the Teddies and Toys shop except the tick tock of the big clock behind the counter. The clock began to bong. It was midnight, the magic time. Suddenly, on the 12th bong, the holiday toys in the front window came alive. They were so excited to see one another. It had been almost a year since they had been out of their boxes. After the toys had greeted each other,

Monkey shouted, "Oh, no! She's missing!"

"Who's missing?" asked Elf. And Monkey
pointed to the empty space.

"She's missing. She's missing,"
sighed Teddy.

"Oh, dear! Oh, dear!" said Mrs. Mouse.
"Maybe Mr. McAndrew just forgot
to take down her box."

"Let's go find her,"
said Jolly Clown.

The five toys ran to the back room where Mr. McAndrew kept his holiday decorations. "So many boxes," said Teddy. "Where do we begin?"

The toys searched and searched and searched. They opened every box—looked in every corner—and looked on every shelf, but she wasn't there. Jolly Clown began to sniffle, and Teddy's eyes began to tear.

"She's gone. She's gone," cried Mrs. Mouse. "Mr. McAndrew must have thrown her away by mistake."

It began to get light outside. The first rays of morning shone on the new-fallen snow.

"Quick," said Elf, "we must get back into the window. The magic time is almost over. Mr. McAndrew will be here soon."

As the toys scurried from the back room past Mr. McAndrew's office, they heard a faint cry. "Help! Help!"

"That's her voice," shouted Monkey.

"Where? Where is she?" asked Teddy.

"In there," said Mrs. Mouse pointing to the office.

The toys ran into the office. They looked all around, and then they looked up.

"There she is!" exclaimed Jolly Clown. And he pointed to a dusty box on the very top shelf of Mr. McAndrew's tall, tall bookcase.

There, peeping out of the box, was . . .
Angel. Mr. McAndrew had misplaced her in all
the commotion of putting away the decorations
last year. Somehow she had been put on the shelf
with the broken toys.

"I can't
get down,"
cried Angel.
"Please help me."

Quick as a wink
Monkey climbed up to the
top shelf of the tall bookcase.
Hanging by his tail, he lifted
Angel out of the box, and
then he carried her down.
The toys were so happy to see
Angel. They dusted her off
and straightened out her
wings and halo.

90

"Hurry, hurry!"
said Teddy, as he led
the toys back to the front
window. "Mr. McAndrew
will be here any moment."

Elf jumped up on the mantle and grabbed his hammer. Mrs. Mouse picked up her broom. Teddy climbed to the top of the ladder. Jolly Clown climbed on the ladder, too, and held a red ball to the tree. Monkey carried Angel and gently placed her on the very top of the tree. Then he swung by his tail over to his rope and picked up the green bell. Just as Monkey held out the bell, Mr. McAndrew came into sight. He was walking very fast, and he had a big smile on his bearded face. Mr. McAndrew had just remembered what it was that he had forgotten . . . Angel.

Without even looking in the front window, Mr. McAndrew quickly opened the front door and hurried to the back room. He searched for Angel's box, but he couldn't find it. He looked in every corner—he looked on every shelf. He even looked behind the drapes. But he couldn't find Angel. Mr. McAndrew was sad. *Where can she be?* he asked himself.

Just then he heard the doorbell jingle. He went to the front of the store, but no one was there. He opened the door, but no one was out-

side. As he turned his head, he caught the reflection of something shining on the very top of the tree in the window.

"There she is," exclaimed Mr. McAndrew. "There's my Angel. I don't remember putting her there. I thought she was missing. And who rang the doorbell?" The puzzled man shook his head as he went back into the store.

The toys winked at each other. They knew what had happened, and so do you. It was the magic of the holidays!

Happy Holidays

Holiday lights and holiday sights,

Holiday gifts bringing cheer,

Each in its way, coming to say,

"Let's have a wonderful year!"

—Virginia H. Niles

95